Clifford

THE ICE RACE

by Apple Jordan
Illustrated by Josie Yee
Based on the Scholastic book series
"Clifford The Big Red Dog"
by Norman Bridwell

ISBN 0-439-69043-9

10 9 8 7 6 5 4 3   05 06 07 08

Printed in the U.S.A.
First printing, January 2005

SCHOLASTIC INC.

New York   Toronto   London   Auckland   Sydney
Mexico City   New Delhi   Hong Kong   Buenos Aires

It was a cold day
on Birdwell Island —
perfect for this year's
dogsledding race!

Clifford and his friends

were the hometown team,

the Island Heroes.

Everyone warmed up.

T-Bone squatted.

Cleo touched her toes.

Mac stretched.

Clifford ate

power biscuits.

The Mighty Huskies

marched to the starting line.

"They look tough,"

said T-Bone.

"But they don't look
like they're having fun,"
said Cleo.

Emily Elizabeth saw

that the Island Heroes

felt nervous.

She began to chant,

"We can do it!

Yes, we can!"

"On your mark . . .

get set . . .

GO!"

The race was on!

A strong wind blew

Emily Elizabeth's map

onto the frozen lake.

"Oh, no!" she cried.

T-Bone carefully

skated onto the lake.

He grabbed the map

and slid back to land.

"Good dog, T-Bone!"

said Emily Elizabeth.

Soon everyone felt hungry.

The Island Heroes

stopped for lunch.

"Oh, no!"

cried Emily Elizabeth.

"The lunches fell

out of the sled."

Emily Elizabeth

had chocolate in her pocket.

But the dogs

couldn't eat that.

Then Mac dug up bones

he had buried last fall!

Each dog had an icy treat.

The team came to

a fork in the road.

They turned left.

Soon they had lost

the trail of the race course!

They were off the map!

Clifford lifted Emily Elizabeth

up to the top of the lighthouse.

She saw the finish line.

The Island Heroes

raced as fast as they could.

But the team

was losing steam.

Clifford slowed down.

T-Bone slowed down.

Cleo and Mac did, too.

"We can do it!"

cried Emily Elizabeth.

"Yes, we can!"

All the dogs got a second wind.

The Mighty Huskies

were only a few yards

from the finish line.

The Island Heroes

ran faster to catch up.

Cleo closed her eyes.

She couldn't bear to look.

With one last,

long stride from Clifford,

the Island Heroes won!

The crowd went wild!

The Mighty Huskies

congratulated them.

"You make racing look fun."

"That's because it is!"

said Clifford.

Everyone had fun celebrating!

Do You Remember?

Circle the right answer.

1. What is the name of Clifford's team?
   a. The Hometown Hounds
   b. The Island Heroes
   c. The Mighty Huskies

2. What did the wind blow onto the lake?
   a. Emily Elizabeth's hat
   b. Emily Elizabeth's scarf
   c. Emily Elizabeth's map

Which happened first?
Which happened next?
Which happened last?

Write a 1, 2, or 3 in the space after each sentence.

Clifford lifted Emily Elizabeth onto the lighthouse. _____2_____

The hometown team's lunches fell out of the sled. _____3_____

Clifford's team took a wrong turn. _____1_____